AVADHĀNA TRADITION IN ODISHA

Prateek Pattanaik

KHANNA BOOK PUBLISHING CO. (P) LTD.
Publisher of Engineering and Computer Books
4C/4344, Ansari Road, Darya Ganj, New Delhi-110002
Phone : 011-23244447-48 **Mobile:** +91-9910909320
E-mail : contact@khannabooks.com
Website: www.khannabooks.com

Dear Readers,

To prevent the piracy, this book is secured with HIGH SECURITY HOLOGRAM on the front title cover. In case you don't find the hologram on the front cover title, please write us to at contact@khannabooks.com or whatsapp us at +91-99109 09320 and avail special gift voucher for yourself.

Specimen of Hologram on front Cover title:

Moreover, there is a SPECIAL DISCOUNT COUPON for you with EVERY HOLOGRAM.

How to avail this SPECIAL DISCOUNT:

Step 1: Scratch the hologram
Step 2: Under the scratch area, your "coupon code" is available
Step 3: Logon to www.khannabooks.com
Step 4: Use your "coupon code" in the shopping cart and get your copy at a special discount
Step 5: Enjoy your reading!

Thanks,
Khanna Publishing House

Price: ₹ 99.00

ISBN: 978-93-5538-441-6

Avadhana Tradition in Odisha
by Prateek Pattanaik

First Edition: 2025

To view complete list of books, please scan the QR Code:

Originally Published by:
Indian Knowledge Systems Division
Ministry of Education

Exclusively Published & Distributed by:
Khanna Book Publishing Co. (P) Ltd.
4C/4344, Ansari Road, Daryaganj,
New Delhi (INDIA)

Visit us at: www.khannabooks.com
Write us at: contact@khannabooks.com

Printed in Bharat.

Contents

Introduction

In the vibrant history of India's cultural and intellectual heritage, the tradition of Avadhana in Odisha stands as a lesser-explored yet profoundly rich chapter. Rooted in simultaneous handling across subjects and an intensive depth of knowledge, Odisha's Avadhana tradition is a unique amalgamation of intellectual prowess and cultural nuances. This book, titled "Avadhana Tradition in Odisha" endeavors to unravel the historical, cultural, and individual dimensions of this exceptional practice.

While Avadhana is celebrated across the Indian subcontinent, the Odisha tradition distinguishes itself through its distinct categories of Avadhana, each demanding a unique level of expertise. The rare 100 Abadhana, alongside the more common 8, 10, 12, and 18 Abadhanas, forms a compelling aspect of Odisha's Avadhana landscape. Furthermore, the book seeks to shed light on extraordinary memorizers called Srutidhara-s who epitomize the intellectual acumen embedded in this tradition.

Eminent Avadhanis of Odisha, such as Upendra Bhanja and Kabibhusana Gopinatha Patra, have played pivotal roles in preserving and advancing this cultural gem. Through meticulous examination, the book will showcase the finer classifications within Sangitavadhana, revealing how poetry, mathematics, games, and concentration converge in a harmonious symphony.

The book's rationale extends beyond mere documentation. It aims to explore the meticulous examination process, the rigorous tests in each subject, and the unique role of Mukti Mandapa pandits as high supervisors, offering readers a comprehensive understanding of the intricate Avadhana tradition of Odisha. Moreover, the flexibility in language choice—Sanskrit, Odia, or both-further distinguishes Odisha's Avadhana practices.

As the reader delves into the pages of this book, they are taken through the multilingual, multilayered world of Odisha's Avadhana. The meticulous examination of subject-wise tests, the integration of theory and application, and the extraordinary Avadhana experiences will collectively weave a narrative that not only preserves the tradition's legacy but also invites a renewed appreciation for the intellectual and cultural finesse intrinsic to Odisha's Avadhana tradition.

Chapter 1
Historical Context of Avadhana in Odisha

Tracing the roots of Avadhana in Odisha, emphasizing its historical significance and cultural integration.

The word Abadhana in Odia refers to extraordinary achievement in a particular subject.

In Odia, Abadhana kariba 'to do abadhana' means to pay attention. Hence, Abadhana refers to single-minded attention towards a discipline. One who has acquired such exceptional skill is referred to as an Avadhani. Depending on the number of disciplines in which skill is acquired, the titles of Astabadhani, Dasabadhani, Dwadasabadhani or Satabadhani were granted by Kings or Mahantas.

The word Abadhana was also used within a different context. The education system of ancient Odisha involved village schools called Chatasalis where the chief teacher would be called an Abadhana. Traditionally, the Abadhanas belonged to a class of people known as the Matibansa. The Matibansa Abadhanas were considered the traditional tutors on puranic grounds. They were the ones who would teach the Odia alphabet first then proceed towards higher education. They taught a variety of disciplines, from vyakarana to ganita to sangita. Traditional education had its own methodology and pedagogy which was holistic and spanned across disciplines, educating students about the basics of multiple subjects.

Traditional examinations of knowledge were conducted in the royal courts of the erstwhile princely states of Odisha and in the Mukti Mandapa of Puri. Titles granted by the Gajapati were considered valid throughout the state. The geographical extent of cultural Odisha extended beyond the borders of the present-day Odisha, which in 1936 became the first Indian state to be formed on linguistic basis. The cultural Odisha however included parts of present-day West Bengal, Madhya Pradesh and Andhra Pradesh, comprising several smaller kingdoms. In the 19th-20th centuries due to several socio-political factors, the courts of Southern Odisha took lead in preserving the ancient tradition of *Abadhana*.

Chapter 2
Varied Avadhana Categories in Odisha

Delving into the distinct Avadhana categories prevalent in Odisha - 8, 10, 12, and the rare 18 Avadhanas, with a glimpse into the exceptionally rare 100 Avadhana.

Quite unique to Odisha is the practice of encompassing an entire discipline under a single *Abadhana*. Hence an *Astabadhani* in Odishan tradition would have to prove his mastery in eight different disciplines through meticulously curated examinations testing 64 sub-disciplines. There would be several examiners in each of the 64 sub-disciplines, the division at each level being exponential. Therefore the Odishan tradition does not identify *Astabadhana* based on the number of examiners; rather it takes into account the number of disciplines; hence, *Kabyabadhana* (allied to *Sahityavadhana* in other regions) is considered just one *Abadhana*, and the number of chief examiners is mandated by convention to be at least eight, accompanied by another eight sub-examiners. Each discipline thus took a week of questioning, spanning upto eighteen hours in a single day.

He who passes an *Astabadhan*a would therefore have to undergo examinations in eight disciplines such as *Sangita, Kabya, Veda, Jyotisha, Vyakarana, Darsana, Ganita,* etc. Through this method, the Odishan tradition would test not just the examinee's ability to answer spontaneously and divide his attention between several disciplines, but also the depth in each subject. In other words, the Odishan Abadhana tradition was multidimensional, testing the examinee both vertically and horizontally in a pedagogical method that was special to this part of the country.

Due to this wider understanding of the term, individual abadhanas were not uncommon, such as the *Sangitabadhana* for musicians. The title of *Sangitabadhani* itself was subdivided into eight subdisciplines of vocal music, instrumental music on both melodic and percussive instruments, song-composition and more. These sub-*Abadhanas* could also be conducted if the individual wishes to do so; an example would be the *Talabadhana*, which consisted only of mastery over the rhythmic aspects of music. In light of this, to be an *Abadhani* in a single discipline also required great command; which is why the title of *Satabadhani* is very rare to come across in Odisha.

Chapter 3
Notable Avadhanis of Odisha

Profiling eminent Avadhanis including Upendra Bhanja, Chandu Rayaguru, Kabisurjya Baladeba Ratha, Kabibhusana Gopinatha Patra, Dasarathi Kabichandra, and Tarini Charan Patra, showcasing their contributions to the Avadhana tradition.

Very little information is known about the Avadhanis of ancient Odisha. However, some of the Avadhanis of yore have been documented in the written accounts of the nineteenth and twentieth centuries. Drawing upon these sources, we can compile an account of the notable Avadhanis of Odisha.

Upendra Bhanja (1670-1740)

One of the medieval Odishan Avadhanis known was Kavi Samrat Upendra Bhanja (1670-1740), born in the royal family of Ghumusara, a princely state in Southern Odisha now in the Ganjam district. Upendra Bhanja is known to have been a Satabadhani according to tradition. In his works are seen glimpses of his mastery over kabya, vyakarana, purana, jyotisa, sangita, kamasastra and several other disciplines. One of his close aides was Swetabahana Bhanja who was a Srutidhara, that is he could reproduce verbatim whatever he had heard once.

The works of Upendra Bhanja display such incredible mastery and skill that it is rare to find a parallel even in the whole country. This is the reason he was known as Pum-Saraswati or Purusha-Saraswati in Odisha; his command over several disciplines and their integrated presentation in his creations were unsurpassed in their time and will remain so for the times to come.

'Chayani' Chandrasekhara 'Chandu' Rayaguru (active ~1736-1793)

Born in the Biranarasinghapura Sasana village near Puri and belonging to the famed Batsasa clan, Chandrasekhara Rayaguru was widely revered for his formidable intellect and miraculous powers. His clan had produced several great minds such as Jivadeva (Preceptor of Gajapati Prataparudra) and Bardhana Rajaguru Mahapatra (author of Durgotsava Chandrika). He earned the title 'Chayani' from the 'Chayana' Vedic ritual. He had achieved siddhi in the worship of the Dasa Mahavidyas and used his talents for the benefit of the public, writing several commentaries on the texts of ancient poets. Chandrasekhara's stories survive in the village, where he is remembered as an Astadasa Abadhani. His extant works include a Nataka named Madhuraniruddha and possibly a tika of Naishadha-Kavya.

Rayaguru was an advisor of the Gajapati king and was awarded with a prized breed of horse called Chakrabaka Aswa, Navaratna Mani Kundala (earrings studded with the nine jewels) and three Gunthuni Hati, a kind of pygmy elephant. Every morning Rayaguru travelled to Puri on the elephant to have a darsana of Lord Jagannatha, indulging in charity along the way.

According to oral accounts, Rayaguru's mother developed a disease in the eye that was believed to have only one remedy : the ash of gajamukta (pearl found in the head of an elephant). Rayaguru went to the Puri court to ask for a gajamukta, but the Gajapati Birakisora Deba (1736-93 reign) blurted out "Let her spend her few remaining days in peace" ; offended by this, Rayaguru left denying the gift and started a puja of the Dasa Mahavidyas for a solution. It is said that Birakisora Deba went insane at one point after which his dethronement became essential for the management of the state, and so as the royal preceptor Rayaguru sought the help of the Peshwa. Apart from this, the goddess is said to have told him to go to the Peshwa court at Pune for the pearl. And so Rayaguru travelled to Pune, finally reaching the main gate of the Peshwa's palace. A huge drum kept at the entrance was supposed to be played by any Pundit who wished an audience with the Peshwa; Rayaguru began playing it recklessly, inviting attention from the sentry who informed him that the each stroke on the drum meant a request for an exam in one discipline and that nobody till date had played eighteen strokes. Rayaguru would have to prove his mettle in eighteen disciplines, which he did. Only in the field of Nyaya he sought the help of Biswanatha, his brother, who was a great Naiyayika.

Among the questions presented in the court, the first question belonged to the discipline of Jyotisa. The Peshwa asks the court, "At what time will the calf be born - what will be the color and gender?". The great Jyotisa pundits in the Peshwa's court answer white and male but Rayaguru says black and female 'gosu krsnā bahuksīrā' – by the Goddess' grace Rayaguru is correct and proves his great learning in the court. The Peshwa devotes himself to Rayaguru, who over time demonstrates several miracles such as walking with a lamp in a thunderstorm and controlling hundreds of snakes at once. The Peshwa rewarded him handsomely, with Banarasi silks, golden ornaments and 108 Salagrama stones.

One of the parting tales of his life describes the sight of Rayaguru stumbling upon the Goddess leaving his home. The goddess complains that he has no offspring, so she will be left with no one to take care of her in the future. Rayaguru reasons that one who passes away in Puri needs no son for moksha; what use is a son, when he has no interest in keeping his name and fame alive? The temple of Bhagabati since then has been in the village, at the very place where Rayaguru convinced the goddess to stay.

Kabisurjya Baladeba Ratha (1789-1845)

The famed Odissi composer-poet Kabisurjya Baladeba Ratha belonged to a family of highly educated Pandits in Ganjam. According to the traditional oral histories passed down by Biswanatha Rayaguru, Kabisurjya's son to Acharjya Tarini Charan Patra, Kabisurjya was awarded the title of Dwadasabadhani for his expertise in the fields of Kabitwa, Sangita and the Vedangas.

Kabibhusana Gopinatha Patra (18th century)

Dasabadhani Kabibhusana Gopinatha Patra is known as the author of several works, the most notable among them being Kavichintamani, a manual of poetics. Gopinatha Patra was based in Paralakhemundi, a royal center of Odisha renowned for its musicianship. Born in a karana clan, Gopinatha Kabibhusana was skilled in the art of singing and instrumental music. He has also authored an Odia kabya by the name Ramachandra Bihara. In the tradition of Paralakhemundi, Gopinatha Kabibhusana is known to have been a Dasabadhani.

Dasarathi Kabichandra (18??-1886)

Based in Banapur, Dasarathi Kabichandra was one of the most famous Abadhanis of nineteenth-century Odisha. His birth date is unknown. Kabichandra was known for his extraordinary skill in Sanskrit and his ability to compose extempore verse. Dasarathi Kabichandra was known for displaying the art of Astabadhana in and outside Odisha in Bengal, Bihar, Rima, Darbhanga and other places.

Dasarathi Kabichandra spent significant time in Khallikota, after which he took shelter in the royal court of Bamanda presided by King Basudeb Sudhaldev. In the words of Kabibara Radhanath Ray,

"Those who have not seen Dasarathi Kabichandra live can never truly realise the extent of his abilities through mere prose. He was an Astabadhani Pandita. His incredible Astabadhani demonstrations were seen by many in Cuttack and Puri. Only those who know Sanskrit and can savour Sanskrit poetry were able to understand Dasarathi Kabichandra's immense power of intellect."

The newspaper Nabeen in a column in 1914 wrote that Dasarathi could understand and speak in Sanskrit, Odia, Bengali. He coud repeat Persian and English as it is during his Abadhana

Gadadhara Bidyabhusana (1859-1944)

Born in 1859 at Manjusha in erstwhile Ganjam, Gadadhara was the second son of Pt Ballabha Narayana. At a very young age he was trained in Sanskrit by Pt Markandeya Mahapatra Sastri who took him to Puri. He then trained under the renowned Odishan astronomist Mahamahopadhyaya Chandrasekhara Singha Samanta, popularly known as Pathani Samanta (1835-1904), becoming his most prominent disciple.

Gadadhara received initiation in the mantra of the goddess Kali, granting him great intellectual prowess. He adorned the courts of Manjusa, Jarada, Budharasingi in Ganjam as a scholar and composed works like 'Rasika Sekhara Bhana' and 'Chandeswara Stotram'. He was awarded the title of 'Bidyabhusana' by the king of Manjusha. Gadadhara Bidyabhusana then went to the court of Chikiti, renowned for music and literature. Here he was awarded the title of 'Astabadhani' for his skill in the eight arts of 1. ślokapātha (citing slokas) 2. ākalana (calculation) 3. apathita ślokapātha 4. śloka rachanā (composing slokas) 5. bādānubāda tarka (debate) 6. praśnottara (answering tricky questions) 7. mantrajapa (chanting mantras) and 8. ayurveda. He demonstrated these at the court of Dharakote and later at Mathura, where he earned the epithets of 'Bidyamaharnaba' and 'Siddhanti'. He also had the titles of 'tarkabagisa' (awarded by Basudeba Sudhaladeba, king of Bamanda), 'kabiraja' (Badakhemundi court), 'kabiratna' (Nayagarh court), 'banibhushana' (Khallikote court) and 'mahamahopadhyaya' (Andhra University).

In his professional career, he served as the vice chancellor of the Sanskrit University of Mathura. His works include : rasikaśekhara bhāna, śankitaśatamanyu, vigambitavijainah (Nātaka), vyaktisañjīvanī (Dhwani), śaktivādah (Nyaya), siddhāntadarpanab tīkā (commentary, Jyotisa), chandeśwara-stotram, navaratnamālā, smrtiśatakam (Smrti) in Sanskrit ; Bisnupurāna, Bānāsura Kābya, Uddhabadūta Chautiśā and Mohanā Chautiśā in Odia.

Tarini Charan Patra (1893-1979)

Astabadhani Acharjya Tarini Charan Patra (1893-1979) was one of the foremost Gurus of Odissi music in 20th-century Odisha. Based in Kabisurjyanagar, he was widely known as a vocalist, composer, scholar and Binakara par excellence.

Patra was born in Ganjam in 1873. He began his musical training first from his elder brother, who taught him Odissi, Chhanda, Champu and the various facets of Odissi music. He then continued higher training (in vocal and Bina) under Guru Gaurahari Mahapatra of Pailipada, Bhanjanagar. Drawn towards Vaishnava practices, Patra developed a dispassionate attitude (vairagya) towards worldly affairs and started a Sankirtana group called 'Bhaja Gobinda'. Soon his fame as a singer spread across Ganjam, with multiple students learning from him and branches of Bhaja Gobinda being established in various places.

For his mastery over eight disciplines he was awarded the title of Astabadhani by the Khallikote rajasabhā after almost a month of rigorous tests, conditions of which included minimal sleep and continuous demanding performances. The title made him famous across Ganjam, and several kings such as the king of Dharakote invited him to their courts, where Patra learned under the veteran court musicians, such as Gayakaratna Binayak Panda of Dharakote, Gayaka Siromani Apanna Panigrahi of Paralakhemundi, Rajaguru Basudeba Mahapatra of Chikiti and Tripati Gayakaratna of Badakhemundi among others. Patra also learned from Guru Mohana Panda of Paralakhemundi and Guru Hadu Patra of Boirani.

In 1940, he established an institution called Sangita Kalamandira at his hometown Boirani (now Kabisuryanagar) for imparting systematic education in Odissi music. At the time, it was the first music institute in all of South Odisha. Patra is the author of several books on Odissi music, the best-known of them being Odisi Sangita Prakasa (1970) which propounded the theory of 32 melas for scientific classification.

In the first half of the 20th century, Patra began systematic efforts to collect original compositions of the ancient poet-composers such as Kabisurjya and Gopalakrusna from their authentic sisya paramparā (disciples), among the last-living masters of the 19th century. Patra laid great emphasis on singing the songs exactly as the composers had taught them, trying to document them in as much detail as he could, in the process collecting and teaching antique forms of ragas along with ancient compositions dating back to as early as the 16th century and archaic methods of binyāsa or elaboration based on six angas of the prabandha, known as sadanga ālāpa. His learning and research was mostly in the kingdoms of South Odisha, undivided Ganjam : Paralakhemundi, Ghumusara, Dharakote, Athagada, Khallikote, Chikiti, Surangi, Badakhemundi (Digapahandi), Sanakhemundi, Jalantara, Manjusa, Tekkali (Tikili), Tarala, Jeypore (Jayapura) ; covering parts of present-day Ganjam, Gajapati, Koraput, Rayagada, Malkangiri, Nabarangpur, Kandhamal, Nayagarh districts. For his efforts, he received the Odisha Sangeet Natak Akademi award in 1972.

Chapter 4
Fine Classifications in Sangitavadhana

Unraveling the intricacies of Sangitabadhana, exploring classifications such as Gitavadhana, Vadyavadhana, Talavadhana, and Vaggeyakara-avadhana.

The Sangitabadhana was also known as the Gandharbabadhana because Sangita was known as the Gandharva Veda, an Upaveda of the Sama Veda. The Sangitabadhana thus consisted of eight conventional sub categories :

Gita - vocal music. Command over several hundreds of ragas, both popular and rare; elaboration or bistara / binyasa of the raga and prabandha using traditional melodic and rhythmic techniques; identification of ragas based on minimal phrases; knowledge of rare compositions; impromptu recall of compositions by a specific composer, in a specific raga or tala with multiple constraints; justification of apparent apabadas or aberrations by tarka based on older prabandhas.

Sastra - theoretical music. Knowledge of the various sastras and justification of various sastric viewpoints based on citations. Some of the Sastras that were considered necessary were Naradiya Siksa, Kohaliya Siksa, Dattilam, Natya Sastra, Sangita Ratnakara, Narada Samhita, Gita Govinda, Sangita Sara, Gita Prakasa, Sangita Narayana, Sangita Damodara, Sangitarnaba Chandrika, Natya Manorama, Sangita Sarani and more.

(Prabandha) Rachana / Baggeyakara - song composition based on ordained constraints. The more difficult aspects included literary techniques of dattachyutakhyara, chitrakabya, specific types of alankara, while also obeying musical constraints of swarartha, composition of specific types of sastric prabandhas

Badya - Tata - string instruments such as bipanchi bina and naradi bina. This was considered one of the most difficult parts of the Sangitabadhana because finer distinctions in the microtonal sruti and swara that had to be demonstrated on the Bina.

Badya - Anaddha - percussive instruments such as mardala and mrudanga. Primarily consisted of rhythmic expertise through the techniques of tala chhindana and kala-ansa-mana, rare talas such as the marga talas and astottara-sata talas, command over the techniques of prastara, ukutana or the ability to play vocal phrases on percussion, composition of sabda using percussive sounds, antargati or simultaneous maintenance of unsimilar rhythmic cycles, demonstration using gini of ekahasta playing. This sub-category was by itself referred to as Talabadhana and was a common practice among the percussionists of Odisha.

Badya - Susira - wind instruments such as bansi and mahuri. The nada of such instruments is believed to be a unique mix of human and instrumental input hence a mid-point between singing and instrumental music, which is why the Susira Badyas are considered a separate test.

Nrutya - dance and abhinaya

Natya - drama and theatrical expression.

Chapter 5

Tests and Practices in Avadhana Subjects

Providing a detailed account of tests in each subject, from singing and vocal music to veena and swara vadyas, rhythmic tests, and on-the-spot song composition.

Certain question patterns from the Sangitabadhana of Acharjya Tarini Charan Patra are known and serve as good examples of the kind of questions asked in the Abadhana Tradition of Odisha. Some of these have been listed below, collected from the sisya-parampara of the venerable Acharjya.

1. Gita or vocal music was the first of the eight sub-categories of the Sangitabadhana. In this round of tests, the examinee was expected to perform several categories of improvisation techniques according to the parampara and sastra of Odissi classical music. This involved a variety of techniques, such as :

    b. Sadanga Alapa : Exploration of the raga through the six angas of akara, tenaka, pata, sloka, gadya and bachanika. Akara involved expansion of the raga through the syllable 'a'; Tenaka consisted of syllables Te, Na, Nom, Ri, etc. which were considered auspicious; Pata consisted of rhythmic syllables such as ta, tari, jham, jhena, etc. replicating the sound of percussion; Sloka consisted of singing metric Sanskrit poetry; Gadya consisted of prose, either in Odia or in Sanskrit, as in the Kisorachandrananda Champu and Bachanika meant alapa through song-lyric but without tala. A mastery over these six limbs of alapa was considered the mark of a purnanga gana, complete singing

c. Bistara / Binyasa : adding layers onto the singing of the prabandha (gita) through improvisation techniques that are either swaratmaka (swara-driven), ragatmaka (raga-driven), chhandatmaka (metre-driven), talatmaka (tala-driven) or misratmaka (complex, consisting of combination of the above).

d. Based on the laya, the tananga improvisation technique wasfurther divided into a variety of tanas such as rekha-tana, kuta-tana with several intricate subtypes such as bartula-tana, nagapasa-tana, meghanada-tana, nandighosa-tana, gomutra-tana, latajala-tana, jaladhi-tana, trigati-tana, susumna-tana and more. A combination of these tana categories was extremely challenging. The tanas could also end at atita, anagata or sama grahas, further complicating things.

2. Sastra or theoretical aspects of music involved questioning about the concepts of Nada, Swara, Jati, Grama, Murchhana, Tana, Raga, Rasa, Bhaba, Anga, Tala, Marga Tala and more. The resolution of conflict between one or more Sastras or the explanation of rare antiquated forms with reference to the traditional Tikas was the subject of questioning in this.

3. (Prabandha) Rachana / Baggeyakara - song composition based on ordained constraints. This was considered separate from kabitwa because of its focus on musical aspects, such as :

   a. swarartha prabandha, mandating the coincidence of the melodic notation with the lyric of the song, meaning the swara-notation itself has to carry meaning.

   b. suda prabandha, cycling through multiple talas. The challenges offered were to compose this kind of prabandha cycling through a variety of ragas as well while ensuring each section of the prabandha reflected pre-assigned descriptive categories.

   c. bikata prabandha, requesting Abadhani to compose a prabandha using elements that cannot be harmonised without great skill. For example, the Abadhani would be requested to compose a prabandha on a given topic using a raga that would be most unsuitable for it. They could similarly add the constraints of rasa, tala and chhanda while the Abadhani would have to come up with a composition and justify it using sastric arguments

d. rare prabandha types such as panchatala and singhanandana, with the aforementioned constraints.

e. literary devices such as jamaka and anuprasa with an onomatopoeic effect in mind, replicating certain alankara structures. The poetic constraints of antarlipi, bahirlipi, anuprasa, jamaka, slesa, chitrakabya and other techniques that also formed a part of Kabyabadhana. Multiple rules imposed at once can be extremely challenging. A rare technique is that of Akhyara Manasa in which stanzas are sung and the listener is supposed to think of a letter (akhyara) in mind. Then the listener reveals the stanzas in which the letter occurred. The Abadhani then has to identify the letter. The original text of the manasa song is written by Abadhana following strict rules which enable them to do so later. For example, if a manasa song having five stanzas is written and the listener has the letter 'ka' in mind, they have to state the stanzas in which the letter occurs: say 1, 3 and 5. Then the Abadhani can identify the letter based on the stanza numbers.

4. Badya - Tata - primarily consisted of :

a. Discussions and demonstrations on the nature of sruti, swara, grama, murchhana, raga, tana and gamaka. The microtonal sruti is considered impossible to perceive by the human ear and hence the Bina is held as the instrument that can measure it, achieving an impossible task and enhancing the limits of human conscience

b. Challenging displays of the bama and dakhina hastabhedas, consisting of guna chalana and kara sarana. This was tested to its limits in the playing of tenaka segments on the Bina while obeying constraints imposed.

5. Badya - Anaddha - percussive instruments such as mardala and mrudanga. Primarily consisted of rhythmic expertise through the techniques of :

   a. Tala chhindana and kala-ansa-mana, to augment the mana or concluding rhythmic segment in such a manner that it falls on the guru akhyara, the first letter of the prabandha, which has been the tradition in Odissi music.

   b. Command over rare talas such as the marga talas and maintaining their tala through elaborate marga kriyas. The astottara-sata talas consisting of several rare talas no longer in widespread use was also tested.

   c. Command over the techniques of prastara, which has a lot to do with the subject of Ganita.

   d. Ukutana or the ability to play vocal phrases on percussion and the composition of sabda using percussive sounds of various instruments such as Mardala, Mrudanga,

   e. Antargati or the ability to keep track of several dissimilar talas at once using various parts of the body. Talabadhani Ganapati Routa from Gurandi, Paralakhemundi mentions his ability of maintaining seven different talas at once using his two hands, two elbows, two feet and by the bobbing of the head. He would light seven dipas and place them on the parts of the body to display his great skill in keeping tala without disturbing the flames. The two shoulders could also be used, increasing the total to nine. Shri Ganapati Routa mentions learning this from his Guru Acharjya Tarini Charan Patra. The process included the involvement of seven/nine taladharas who would keep track of the individual talas as a check.

   f. Demonstration using gini of ekahasta playing. Two pairs of ginis would be wrapped around the palms of the two hands while additional pairs could be held between the teeth or using different fingers.

6. Badya - Susira - wind instruments such as bansi and mahuri. This segment of the examination dealt with the different kinds of playing techniques depending on the fingering.

7. Nrutya - dance and abhinaya, demonstrations of rasa, bhaba, parija, bhangi, chali and other aspects.

8. Natya - drama and theatrical expression. Traditional dramas such as Jagannatha-Vallabha Nataka and Usaniruddha Nataka were considered mandatory parts of this section of the examination.

Chapter 6

Shastra and Prayoga in Odisha's Avadhana Tradition

Analyzing the emphasis on both shastra (theory) and prayoga (application) in Odisha's Avadhana tradition, highlighting the comprehensive approach.

In the Abadhana examination, a comprehensive scholastic approach was considered inevitable. Practical skill and theoretical knowledge were considered the two essential axes for this test. In the absence of the former, no theoretical knowledge would be truly meaningful; in the absence of the latter, the artist would be a mere performer, something that was not considered ideal.

In the field of Sangitabadhana, only singers or Gayakas were considered unfit for the award of Abadhana without appreciation of the Sastras. A knowledge over the Sastras immediately relevant to the discipline was considered a mark of respect towards the ancient tradition and the acharyas of yore. Hence, a mere singer could not be invited to the Sangitabadhana. The Sangita-Sastras were considered essential knowledge.

This approach that balances theoretical and practical knowledge was a chief characteristic of the Odishan Abadhana tradition.

Chapter 7

Multilingual Avadhana and Liberty of Subject Choice

Examining the flexibility of Avadhana in Odisha, where participants could choose subjects in Sanskrit, Odia, or both, fostering a multilingual approach.

In the Odishan tradition, Abadhana tests were conducted either in Odia or Sanskrit, depending on the examinee's choice.

By the 17th century, Odia poets had already proven that the verbal techniques in Sanskrit poetry could be recreated in the local Prakrit, that is Odia, as well. Upendra Bhanja made it amply clear that the Odia language was well-equipped for all possible poetic styles. Apart from recreating Sanskrit poetic techniques in Odia, he also invented as well as took pre-existing indigenous Odia poetic techniques to greater heights.

The Abadhana tradition in Odisha had several pre-existing disciplines under which examinations were conventionally conducted, each having finer classifications into eight sub-disciplines, also by convention. Some of these disciplines were:

- **Vedas** : Rik, Yaju, Sama, Atharva
- **Any of the Vedangas** : Shiksha, Chhandas, Nirukta, Vyakarana, Kalpa, Jyotisha
- **Any of the Upavedas** : Ayurveda, Dhanurveda, Gandharvaveda (Sangita) or Arthasastra
- **Any of the Darshanas** : Nyaya, Vaisheshika, Sankhya, Yoga, Mimamsa, Vedanta

- **Other disciplines** such as Silpa, Chitra, Ganita, Kabya, Byaktakhyara, Chaturanga, Lekhana, Kanthagrahana, Juktikarana and others.

Each of the above disciplines was considered one Abadhana. For example, Gandharva would considered one Abadhana, Chhandas would be considered one Abadhana, and so on. Titles such as Astabadhani or more were granted based on the total number of Abadhanis. The only exception was that Abadhana in the Vedas was considered to be of greater merit compared to the others, and often special titles were awarded to Vedic scholars for distinction, owing to their mastery over the vast corpus of ancillary texts alongside the primary Samhitas.

Chapter 8
The Rigorous Examination Process

Providing insights into the intense examination process, where each subject took 5-7 days, and participants faced questioning from multiple experts for up to 18 hours per day.

The Abadhani only had liberty to choose the disciplines. Each discipline took around a week days of questioning from multiple experts on the subject, upto eighteen hours in a single day. The structure was exponential; for example each of the disciplines of the Astabadhana were subdivided into eight further sub-disciplines. On similar lines, a body of eight Pandits would preside over a group of sixty four questioners for each discipline. Many scholars were themselves Abadhanis and skilled in more than one discipline. Even the lowest Abadhana examination, an Astabadhana examination involved the organiser-king inviting over a hundred Pandits to conduct the intensive questioning.

During Acharya Tarini Patra's Astabadhana examination, over a hundred scholars from across the state were present, including those of the Khallikota court. The external pundits were invited from the neighbouring kingdoms of Dharakota, Badakhemundi, Sanakhemundi, Nayagada, Ghumusara, Khandapada, Jalantara, Manjusa, Chikiti, Surangi, Paralakhemundi and others apart from the Mukti Mandapa of Puri. The Mukti Mandapa pandits were inevitably some of the highest supervisors in any Abadhana conducted in Odisha. Hence, conducting an Abadhana was an extraordinary and costly affair for the king. However, it was seen as a status symbol for the State by the King as well as the public.

The Abadhana examination was a public event and people were free to attend. Due to the long all-night nature of the event, the Abadhani himself would get minimal time for sleep and daily chores. The nature of the event was supposed to test simultaneous attention to multiple disciplines, high competence over each discipline and spontaneous creativity without exhaustion.

Distraction was offered to the Abadhani as well as the general public in the mode of mundane activities such as counting the number of times a cymbal would be rung or counting the number of times a pile of stones would be hit by the general public. The Abadhani was supposed to be immersed in the art as well as aware of their immediate surroundings by this activity, reinforcing simultaneous attention to the external and the inner world at the same time.

Chapter 9
The Role of Mukti Mandapa Pandits

Exploring the unique role of Mukti Mandapa pandits as high supervisors in Odisha's Avadhana examinations.

The Mukti Mandapa is a high seat inside the complex of the Jagannatha Temple of Puri. It is situated in front of the Adi Nrusingha Temple and is essentially a black granite platform almost five feet high, supported by several pillars. This Mandapa is meant to be the seat of the most learned Brahmins from across Odisha, especially the 16 Sasana villages around Puri, considered great centres of learning since ancient times. The Brahmins of the Mukti Mandapa were carefully nominated through a series of rigorous tests and were experts in the matters of Veda, Vedanga, Upanisad, Agama, Puja-Paddhati, Tantra amidst several other topics. Within the Pandits, a higher apex body was further nominated to take the final decision based on discussion.The Mukti Mandapa is named thus because of the traditional belief that the way to Mukti can be attained by the advice of this esteemed body of scholars. The Mandapa is also known as Brahmasana, that is, each scholar who sits on top of it must be as learned as Brahma himself.

The Mukti Mandapa body of scholars formed the fulcrum of the temple ecosystem. Any confusions or disputes regarding the performance of rituals or the resolution of disputes was brought to the notice of the Mukti Mandapa Sabha. The traditional alamanac Panji is also approved by this sabha and only then is considered valid. A meeting would be held and the opinion of the Pandits was held supreme. The Mukti Mandapa performed this role not only for the Jagannatha Temple of Puri but for the entire Odia-speaking regions. From the highest office-holders such as the kings to the common man, the Mukti Mandapa Pandits had the sole duty of providing well-considered advice to maintain the sastric backbone of the society and prevent chaos. In other words, the Mukti Mandapa acted as the highest judicial body for all matters of public interest.

In the Abadhana examinations conducted in ancient Odisha, the presence of Pandits from the Mukti Mandapa was considered mandatory. The apex body of granting the title of an Abadhani was specifically approved by this committee. Once decided, the title would be formally announced by the king in the presence of the Pandits, while the Mukti Mandapa Pandits would mark the occasion with sacred artefacts brought from the Jagannatha Temple of Puri which were offered to the Abadhani as a mark of respect. This usually consisted of Angalagi (cloth which has been offered to Jagannatha earlier) and Nirmalya (dried rice that has been offered as Mahaprasada) along with some Maharda Mala (flower and Tulsi garlands that have been offered earlier). The offering of Jagannatha's sacred artefacts by the Pandits of the Mukti Mandapa marked the formal announcement of the Abadhani title.

Chapter 10

Acharya Tarini Patra's Extraordinary Avadhana

Narrating the extraordinary Abadhana conducted by Acharya Tarini Patra, involving a hundred pundits and the substantial efforts undertaken by the king.

In the 1920s, Tarini Charan Patra was a young musician who had undergone significant training under his elder brother and his Guru Pt. Gourahari Mahapatra. Known for his vairagya and bhakti, he founded several kirtana groups across Southern Odisha and went around singing in his commanding voice, earning him great fame in the villages of the region. Several miraculous incidents record Patra's spiritual attainments, including an incident where Mahaprabhu Jagannatha informed his head priest in a dream that he had "gone away to Boirani to listen to Patra's Kirtana". Patra burst out into a song at the head priest's arrival - "ଆଉ କି ଦେଖିବ ନୟନ ମୋ ବାଇମନ, ବୋଇରଣୀ ଗ୍ରାମ ବଇକୁଣ୍ଠ ଧାମ ହରନାମେ ପରପୂର୍ଣ୍ଣ". Events such as these spread Patra's fame across the state.

Drawn by the incidents and the mystery around this young musician, the king of Khallikota invited him to his court on the suggestion of Sri Sannyasi Kar of Khariamukundapura Sasana. The initial meeting in King Mardaraja's court proved positive and Tarini's effortless execution won over the scholars of the Court. Since Tarini was active in the region controlled by the Khallikot State, the King decided to offer him the title of Astabadhani. The young Patra agreed in a state of nonchalant vairagya.

With over a hundred Panditas in the Khallikota court, Tarini appeared for tests in the eight disciplines of Sangita, Kabitwa, Chaturanga, Lekhana, Ganita, Kanthagrahana, Byaktakhyara and Juktikarana. Since Patra revealed very little about his personal life or achievements himself, little detail is known about the disciplines other than Sangita and Kabitwa in the examination. The exercises in the Abadhana examination in the Sangita and Kabitwa disciplines were later mentioned by Patra to his disciples (Guru Ladu Kishore Pani and Guru Bhubaneswar Senapati) in order to educate them about the necessary practice techniques to achieve extraordinary skill. Patra displayed extraordinary skill in Ganita or mathematics in his day-to-day life, as known from the accounts of his disciples.

After the months-long examination was finished, the group of scholars unanimously agreed on the award of the Astabadhani title, a rare occurrence for the time. This was formally confirmed by the offering of ritual items from the Jagannatha Temple by the Pandits of the Mukti Mandapa. The king of Khallikota offered to him the position of the raja-sangitagya of the Khallikota-Athagada State as a mark of respect. Since Kabisurjya Baladeba Ratha had held this position in the past as the raja-sangitagya of Athagada, Patra accepted this position with great reverence, taking it to be a blessing from the musicians of yore.

After his successful Abadhana at the Khallikota court, Patra was handed over the Bipanchi Bina by his first Guru Gourahari Mahapatra to mark him as the primary successor of the lineage. Patra was also invited by several courts to honur his talent. The king of Dharakota offered Patra golden ornaments such as the makara kundala and khadu, which he denied out of his Vaishnava leanings. In his stays at various courts he learned under the veteran court musicians, such as Gayakaratna Binayak Panda of Dharakote, Gayaka Siromani Apanna Panigrahi of Paralakhemundi, Rajaguru Basudeba Mahapatra of Chikiti and Tripati Gayakaratna of Badakhemundi among others. Patra also learned from Guru Mohana Panda of Paralakhemundi and Guru Hadu Patra of Boirani. He dedicated his life to collecting and documenting ancient compositions of Odissi music from veteran musicians in and around his region and teaching them to students to keep them alive.

Conclusion:

In this monograph, an attempt has been made to analyse the Abadhana tradition as was in vogue in Eastern India, until the late nineteenth and early twentieth centuries, after which the practice seems to have become virtually non-existent in this part of the country. Until then, the art of Abadhana was sustained by the generous patronage of the kings, earning them the name of a good patron as well as the honour of having formidable scholars in their court.

The primary sources for the early Abadhanis of the Odishan stream are all oral accounts faithfully preserved by their artistic lineage or succession of disciples. Many of these oral accounts have also been put to writing in the last two centuries. For the more recent Abadhanis, meticulous newspaper and magazine accounts are reliable sources to draw upon.

Among the Odishan Abadhanis that information could be gathered are the medieval poet-musician Kabi Samrat Upendra Bhanja (1670-1740; Satabadhani), Chayani Chandrasekhara 'Chandu' Rayaguru (active 1736-93; Astadasa Abadhani), poet-musician Kabisurjya Baladeba Ratha (1789-1845; Dwadasabadhani), Kabibhusana Gopinatha Patra (18th century; Dasabadhani), Dasarathi Kabichandra (18??-1886; Astabadhani), Gadadhara Bidyabhusana (1859-1944; Astabadhani) and musician Acharjya Tarini Charan Patra (1893-1979; Astabadhani).

The last examination seems to have been conducted by the Khallikote royal court sometime in the 1940s and the title 'Astabadhani' was awarded to Tarini Charan Patra. Thus, an understanding of the concepts survives till date, especially among the hundreds of disciples that Patra trained, mostly by his own recounting of his experience. Patra was widely referred to by the title, because of the respect the Khallikote court commanded among the general public as well as reflecting the amazement of the people about the very rare test of skill, though Patra himself refrained from using the title due to his Vaishnava sense of humility.

A constant motif in the Odishan Abadhana examinations has been the emphasis laid upon what can be called the 'multidimensional approach', a term referring to the excruciating detail in which the candidate was tested in each subject, resulting in an exponentially more challenging system. This has been pointed out by several scholars and practitioners in the past and seems to be unique to the local tradition. This is also why the practice of Sahasrabadhana does not seem to be as popular in Odisha; the title of Astabadhana itself demands a month of grilling examination divided into sixty-four sub-tests! Satabadhanis are not unheard of in the state, but exceedingly rare.

The involvement of the Muktimandapa of Puri reflects the scale and grandeur of this ancient custom as well as the pan-Odishan importance of the conduct of an Abadhana examination. The Abadhana examinations being seen as the apex of intellectual mastery, the significant role of the Puri scholars and the Gajapati king, especially in the award of the final title in the form of used articles of the deity of Jagannatha himself, indirectly points to the magnitude of the title; an award so precious that only the highest king would be capable of offering it.

The distinct tradition of Abadhana in Odisha thus traces back a rich history of several centuries and is characterised by its unique multidimensional approach, focussing on the twin aspects of versatility as well as depth, immersion as well as alertness and simultaneous yet divided attention.